Bright ≡Summaries.com

Big Brother

BY MAHIR GUVEN

BOOK ANALYSIS

Written by Sarah Ponzo
Translated by Oliver Brown

Big Brother

BY MAHIR GUVEN

MAHIR GUVEN

FRENCH-TURKISH WRITER

- **Born stateless in 1986 in Nantes**
- **Big Brother is his first novel**

A French-Turkish writer born in 1986 in Nantes, Mahir Guven wrote his first novel in 2017. His personal story echoes his writing: born stateless to a Turkish mother and a Kurdish father, he will never stop looking for his place in society, just like the main character of his novel. Critically acclaimed, *Big Brother* won several awards in 2018, including the Prix Première, the Prix Régine Deforges and the Prix Goncourt du Premier roman. The novel's powerful and incisive style, as well as the themes it deals with, have put it in the prestigious world of French literature.

In parallel to this writing job, he participates in the newspaper *Le 1* (a weekly launched in 2014 by Éric Fottorino and Laurent Greilsamer; it deals with current affairs through the eyes of writers, researchers, anthropologists, etc.) which he decided to leave in April 2018 to devote himself to his projects. He is currently a contributor to *America* magazine, launched in 2017 by Éric Fottorino and François Busnel, a French quarterly devoted to the United States during Donald Trump's term of office.

BIG BROTHER

A QUEST FOR IDENTITY IN THE 21ST CENTURY

- **Genre:** novel

- **Reference edition**: *Big Brother*, Paris, Éditions Philippe Rey, 2017, 270 p.

- **1st edition:** 2017

- **Themes:** social integration, suburbs, terrorism, radicalisation, humanitarianism, uberisation, religion

Published in 2017, this first novel has been widely acclaimed by critics, as much for its literary quality as for the accuracy of the themes addressed. Very much rooted in reality, it largely echoes the crises that France is currently experiencing: the rise of terrorism, the uberisation of society and the perpetual quest for social integration.

The story takes place in a suburb of Paris where the atmosphere is poisonous, some time after the attacks on Charlie Hebdo (7 January 2015) and 13 November 2015. The novel is constructed in alternating chapters: those devoted to the older brother and those that focus on the younger brother.

Using the direct style and phrasing so distinctive of suburban youth, Mahir Guven manages to give a particular rhythm to the whole work.

SUMMARY

AN UNEXPECTED RETURN

Big Brother, whose real name is Azad, a VTC Uber driver in Paris, waits for potential clients as he does every day. Between each passenger, the wait is felt and it is an opportunity for him, and indirectly for us, to go back into his past and discover his story. His little brother, called Hakim, has been in Syria for three years as the story begins, officially to participate in a humanitarian project. We quickly understand that Big Brother suspects him of having left France to wage jihad in Syria. A nagging resentment clouds his thoughts: he holds a terrible grudge against his brother for leaving. One evening, while smoking a cigarette after dropping off his client at the bus station in Bagnolet, a bus from Cologne stops not far from him. A group of young people got off and walked towards his car. A young man gets out and gets into a black Citroën; the scene only lasted a few seconds, but Azad is convinced: this man is his brother! He decides to follow the vehicle to find out for sure.

A DIVE INTO THE PAST

After an unsuccessful chase, Azad recalls his childhood and adolescence with this long cherished and now hated brother. They grew up in a Parisian suburb, educated by a father opposed to all forms of religion and a mother who was loving but weakened by illness. One September 8th, when they were still young boys, their mother tragically died after a violent argument between their father and their paternal grandmother, thus putting an end to their childhood. This dramatic death will condition the lives of the two men: one (Azad) will close in on himself and evacuate his grief by adopting the life of a young gangster, while the other (Hakim) decides to study nursing to save lives. Azad, now a drug dealer, is arrested by the police. A deal is struck with one of the policemen: to escape prison, he agrees to become their eyes and ears. As for Hakim, a nurse at the Georges-Pompidou European Hospital in Paris, he meets a surgeon involved in an NGO at a conference and decides to go and do humanitarian work in war-torn countries, particularly in Syria. One evening, someone rings his doorbell: there is no longer any doubt that it is his brother who is facing him.

THE DILEMMA

After the shock of his reunion with his brother, Azad begins to seriously question his motives for returning. Why doesn't he want to see his father after three years of absence? Did he really go to Syria to work as a humanitarian? Why this sudden return to France? All these questions become even more burning when he discusses with a lawyer, the brother of one of his friends from the suburbs, and above all with the policeman with whom he collaborates to make progress in the investigations. If his brother's return to France went unnoticed, it was more than predictable: the lawyer and the policeman warn Azad about the risks he runs in protecting his brother, a fugitive in the eyes of French law. The young man hesitates: should he continue to protect his brother or denounce him to the gendarmerie? Can one deny one's brother, one's own blood, to protect oneself?

THE NECESSARY ESCAPE

After some reflection, Azad decides to believe his brother, even though he still has doubts. So he thinks about how he can save him, and sees no other solution than to flee. He devises a plan: they will go to Portugal, where one of his friends owns a secluded country house, and start over. He plans the exact day and time of the departure. A few days before, when he had put aside his job as a VTC driver to focus on his reunion with his brother, he decided to resume his routine so as not to arouse the suspicions of the police. Indeed, although he has acquired the status of informer, he remains under surveillance. Moreover, he wants to collect as much money as possible for their departure. Azad contacts people he knows in order to obtain a false passport and identity card for his brother. He plans to accompany him to Portugal, then return to France for a while before joining him permanently. But doubts persist as a tragic event is brewing in France, to which his brother may not be totally unrelated.

THE HARSH REALITY

On the day of his departure for Portugal, his brother leaves the house at dawn and steals his car. Azad senses that something is up and fears that his suspicions are correct: his brother is not who he thought he was. He tries to keep working, secretly hoping that his brother will be there that night, but he has a terrible feeling that Hakim is a terrorist. Despite his calls, the young man doesn't pick up… As he sits on a bench in the heart of Paris, not having the courage to work, Azad receives a news alert on his phone: an attack has taken place, a car has exploded. He immediately has the intuition that it is his car, stolen this morning by his brother…

CHARACTER STUDY

BIG BROTHER'S FAMILY

Big Brother

Big Brother, whose real name is Azad, is one of the main protagonists of this novel. He is a young man soon to be thirty years old when the story opens. He works as a VTC Uber driver in Seine-Saint-Denis and lives alone. His dexterity at the wheel has earned him the nickname of Pilot. A former petty thief, he narrowly escapes prison and becomes an informer for the police, and more particularly for a policeman nicknamed Le Gwen. For a long time, the young man lived within the family circle, but after his mother's death, relations with the other members of the family disintegrated. His Friday ritual, from which he cannot deviate, consists in having lunch with his father, with whom the links have become more and more distant since the departure of his younger brother for Syria. His professional and personal life is hardly stable. With no official girlfriend (even though he sees a young girl regularly) and no fixed income, Azad tries as best he can to combine his life in the suburbs with his companions in misfortune with a life in 'classic' society.

Little Brother

He is the second main protagonist. We learn at the end of the novel that his name is Hakim, but everyone calls him Band-Aid because of his work as a nurse. He is Azad's brother and lives in a loving family. Promised a bright future in the hospital environment, he studied nursing and works at the Georges-Pompidou Hospital. However, a bad encounter was to divert him from this well-trodden path. His paternal grandmother taught him the basics of Islam and he quickly discovered a real passion for religion, even though his father had always refused to teach them the slightest prayer. This great enthusiasm for religion brought him closer to the imams in his suburb, who reinforced his idea of defending the Syrian cause. It became more and more obvious to him that he wanted to work for an NGO: he even had an interview with Médecins Sans Frontières. It is during a nursing conference in Strasbourg that he meets Mr. Bedrettin, who will take him to Syria. When the story begins, he has been missing for three years, officially for humanitarian purposes, but doubts remain throughout the novel about his true intentions.

The father

Father of Azad and Hakim, we do not know his first name. Born in Syria into a large family (five sisters and a brother), he fled his country for political reasons: he was putting up posters against the current regime and was caught by the men of Bashar el-Assad's father, Hazef el-Assad, Syrian president from 1971 until his death in 2000. As a punishment, they cut off his finger. A relatively lenient punishment since his older brother disappeared and his cousin was tortured much more violently. He arrived in France in the 1980s to continue his studies. He taught French at the Institut des Langues Orientales, where he met his future wife. He obtained a doctorate despite his broken French and, during the annual summer closure of the university, worked as a night taxi driver. He has a rather conflictual relation-ship with his mother, whom he takes in June 1998 following the conflicts in Syria. A violent argument broke out between them in September over religious issues, and it was on the same day that his wife died. Since then, he has worked as a full-time taxi driver, has his own license plate and is approaching retirement age. He takes a dim view of the fact that his son would rather be an Uber driver than inherit his taxi driver's plate. He firmly believes that his young son Hakim will return from his humanitarian journey.

The mother

We don't know her first name either. We only know that she was French, Breton to be precise, and that she went to Paris to study. She studied at the Institute of Oriental Languages where she met her future husband, who was her teacher at the time. Her mother lives in Saint-Malo where Hakim and Azad used to go regularly as children to spend holidays in the region where they have their roots. She suffers from repeated migraines which suggest a more ferocious illness eating away at her from the inside. Very weakened, she died on 8 September after having calmed her husband down during a violent argument with his mother. She has been dead for more than 18 years when the novel begins and yet she is omnipresent in the story: the reader quickly perceives that this tragic death has conditioned the psychology of the other characters.

The paternal grandmother

Zahié, Azad and Hakim's paternal grandmother, arrives in France in the 1990s following the conflicts raging in her country, Syria. During her stay with her son, she teaches Arabic to her daughter-in-law and the rudiments of Islam to her grandchildren, despite her son's formal prohibition to teach them the religion he "rejects". One morning in September, her son attacks her violently after attending the prayers she makes Aazad and Hakim perform. The same day, her daughter-in-law tragically dies. Her son could no longer look after her full-time, so he decided to put her in a retirement home in the west of Paris. Despite their differences, his son pays her a rather luxurious pension so that she can end her life with dignity, family being a sacred value in their eyes.

BIG BROTHER'S CLOSE CIRCLE

Le Gwen

The Gwen is a policeman with whom Azad has a relationship every first Wednesday of the month. In order to avoid prison, the young man has agreed to provide information on suburban youth gangs, in various drug and burglary cases, but also in the context of possible radicalisation. In exchange for this information, Le Gwen helps Azad when he is faced with delicate situations.

Azad owes him a great deal because it is the policeman who will help him find a job through one of his friends. He will also help him to find social housing by lobbying the administration. He will again help him by not losing his job even though he has no points on his licence. Azad considers him as his second father: he knows everything about his family and his background. So when he talks to him about the possibility of his brother's return, he warns him that he could be considered an accomplice if he does not denounce him.

Mehmet

Mehmet is Azad's best friend, he is Turkish and runs the restaurant *Le 120* where all the taxi drivers meet every day to eat and chat. Azad calls him "Demytho" because he always tells half lies. The information he gives is always partly true and partly false. Moreover, it is Mehmet who warns Azad that a possible terrorist attack is being prepared in the suburbs.

CHARACTERS CLOSE TO LITTLE BROTHER

Bedrettin

He is a member of the NGO *Islam & Peace*, which is giving a lecture on care in war situations at a conference at the Strasbourg Hospital. He spent his childhood in Turkey before arriving in France at the age of seventeen to continue his studies. He passed his baccalaureate at the age of twenty-one and then went on to study medicine. When the war in Syria broke out, he decided to leave his job in Strasbourg to join the NGO *Islam & Peace*, which helps the Syrian population. He became Hakim's mentor when Hakim joined the organisation. Bedrettin also taught him how to be a war surgeon and gave him more and more responsibilities. Shortly after their arrival in Syria Bedrettin deploys to another village, leaving Hakim in charge of the hospital.

Blonde beard

This is a nickname given to him by Hakim, we do not know his real name. It is obviously a variant of Barbarossa, the name attributed to the Ottoman corsair Khizir Khayr ad-Dîn. Blondebeard is the emir who rules the Al-Bab district in Syria, where Hakim will meet with the NGO *Islam & Peace*. He develops a special relationship with Hakim when Hakim saves his sister-in-law during her delivery. He finds him a wife, Leila, and a house. When Bedrettin leaves for Mayadin, a village in western Syria, Blondebeard becomes the official contact for the NGO *Islam & Peace*. He enlists Hakim in missions that go far beyond the work he was supposed to do in Syria: the young man participates as a nurse in murderous commandos. It is also Blondebeard who sends Hakim back to France with a false Syrian passport so that he can carry out attacks on French territory.

KEYS TO READING

THE POWER OF LANGUAGE

The question of language is a key issue in the history of literature. In the course of the 2000s, a so-called 'suburban literature' emerged, of which the novel *Big Brother* is certainly a part.

With the rapid growth of cities in the 19th and 20th centuries, suburbs emerged. From the 1950s onwards, with the arrival of immigrants on French territory, a vocabulary specific to the younger generation developed on the outskirts of the city, which had an impact on the evolution of the French language as well as on literature. Indeed, writers from the Maghrebian immigrant community situate their literary production on the fringes of what is usually done, by resorting to oralised language.

Thanks to the use of this oralised language, which manifests itself in specific elements of language or punctuation marks, the reader has the feeling of being face to face with the characters who populate the novel: "It's been a while since some weird guys showed up near our house. They were really into the mosque. (p. 149)

The author takes care to render the colloquial language peculiar to young people from the suburbs (the verlan) and dialects, a mixture of French and Arabic, which plunge us directly into the heart of this Franco-Syrian family and give it a unique rhythm:

Language is doubly important in this novel as it also appears as a vehicle for identification and integration into society. We see how important French is to the father, even though he speaks it roughly, because it is through learning the language that he was able to integrate in France. On the other hand, as far as Big Brother is concerned, the use of slang denotes this fierce desire to emancipate himself through language: "Sometimes I've been taken for a ride, but you know me, I've lived in 3-5-7. (p. 226)

Such language is used by Mahir Guven to highlight the reality of the environment in which the characters evolve. Indeed, characters from the suburbs, in perpetual search of identity and recognition in the eyes of society, would not have been able to use a "classic" language that would not have been representative of what they live. This is why the author provides a glossary at the end of the book to enable us to appropriate this language which, in many ways, is relatively unknown to us, especially when it comes to Arabic. "Dear readers, to make reading easier for you and to introduce you to the energetic and lively vocabulary of a part of the youth, here is a glossary" (p. 265).

IN SEARCH OF ITS IDENTITY

One of the central themes of this novel is the perpetual quest for identity in the heart of a French society that is not entirely that of the main characters, or at least does not seem to include them as they would wish.

> *"No backbone: not really French, not really Syrian, not really native, not really immigrant, not Christian, not Muslim. They are meteciles without knowing why they are meteciles. My father didn't tell his half of the story, so some episodes are missing and we imagine the rest (...) How can we find our way back when we don't know where we come from?" (p. 72)*

This echoes perfectly what stateless people can feel in any society, not only in France. It is easy to understand how important origin is to these young people from the suburbs. They cannot build themselves properly if they are missing a part of their own history:

> *"All I know is that the guys from the neighbourhoods do what everyone else in this society does, they reproduce the life of their parents. Here, apart from the few rappers and sportsmen, shrubs that hide a forest of robots, we haven't done what we dreamed of doing. Like our parents, rheylito... The world turns, and its balance is perpetual. (p. 100)*

Nevertheless, they are also very lucid about their situation, trying by all means to find their place, notably through work: "(...) It's rotten, Rhey! The suit? It's rotten, Rhey! It stinks of shit, but you have to deal with it, because without it, it's worse. You don't even get respect any more. " (p. 100) Indeed, although Azad is not the 'typical' young Frenchman, he does everything to fit in: he has a flat, works and pays his taxes. He tries to be accepted as best he can in this French society, which is nevertheless very picky about him. This theme of the quest for identity is widely used in literature: everyone knows Shakespeare's famous maxim "To be or not to be" (Shakespeare, Hamlet), which is at the heart of every human being's inner questioning. Identity is acquired through the social context in which we evolve and the relationships we may have with others.

It is interesting to note that this quest for identity, which is close to assimilation into a group, does not concern Azad's father, who does not want to be assimilated or labelled. He is neither Arab nor French, but claims to be a human being above all:

A CURRENT NOVEL

This novel is perfectly anchored in French and international current affairs through the themes it deals with.

Terrorism

The time period in which the story is set is quite significant, and there are regular references to socio-political situations in France and abroad that hint to readers at the novel's contemporary anchorage: "But since *Charlie* and the 13th, we've been called in mostly for terrorist cases." (p. 40). With this remark, we fully understand that he is referring to the terrorist attacks that France suffered in 2015. This is all the more significant for the main character who lives in the suburbs, and the shortcut is very quickly made in people's heads. Especially as he has made mistakes in the past and is in contact with people who may be linked to terrorism. This is why one of his friends warns him: if he doesn't want to be assimilated to these terrorists, he mustn't let himself get involved:

"Brother, don't do strange things. You know that this mosque is the boarding platform for the Cham. (p. 86)

Terrorism is a recurring theme in mainstream literature. Although it is not new, it is increasingly mentioned in post-2015 novels. After the French attacks, a number of novels dealing with the survivors or paying tribute to the victims have appeared. But *Big Brother* is one of the few novels that deals with the departure of a brother for the jihad in such an accurate way. Literature thus becomes a kind of outlet for authors and readers alike to heal their wounds, whether physical or psychological.

An uber society

The disintegrating social situation is quite palpable in this novel, which brings to the forefront questions that have marked society, particularly its uberisation. What is remarkable is that Big Brother is the spokesperson for this new society, a protagonist who accepts all types of work at the risk of undermining a part of the social gains hard won by past generations: "Since Uber and the platforms arrived, they [*taxi drivers*] have lost a lot of fares and customers. Too bad for them. I understand why they are angry, but it's partly their fault." (p. 30); "Uber has understood everything. It's easy to be a customer, it's easy to be a driver." (p. 31)

Nevertheless, he is fully aware of the harm that uberisation is doing to society, and what upsets him even more is that taxi drivers are targeting the wrong people: "But in fact, Uber's bosses are clever, because the taxis are attacking us, the VTC drivers, and not the guys who created the system and maintain it" (p. 32).

Azad's father, on the other hand, appears much more reactionary towards this new technology that conditions the new society: "Life is not complicated. Okay, you work with Uber application, phone, ek jetera. But who is the owner of Uber? You participate in demolishing a profession, taxi for others. If tomorrow, one day, no more taxi, Uber monopoly, it's not good…" (p. 30). He even goes so far as to participate in various taxi driver demonstrations.

The uberisation of society also puts the economy at risk. In this novel, the announcement of the closure of a VTC platform is quite significant of the damage that results from such a working strategy: "We were talking about the new start-ups as the future of the economy and, by domino effect, the future of humanity. So this bankruptcy was an event. The elites of our country, the Minister of the Economy in chief, were voting massively for these new companies and getting all the junkyard dogs like me on board." (p. 172). The uberisation of society also highlights this frantic race for statistics and scores, making human beings slaves to their image: "Some people were already driving for both platforms, but that would require constant gymnastics on the phone, because you could be assigned to two clients at the same time. And when you declined an errand, the bill would go down." (p. 186)

THE RELIGIOUS QUESTION

The question of religion plays an important role in this novel through the character of the little brother. It is the exacerbated practice of religion that is questioned, not religion as such. Indeed, it is when Hakim becomes more and more enclosed in his faith that the danger becomes clear: "As the war progressed, the little one's beard grew." (p. 123). Until one day he ceases all communication with his family and decides to leave: "And one day he left home. To go and live with a friend (...) Three days later, his telephone line had been suspended. After a few weeks without news, we received an email. He had left for a humanitarian mission in Mali for a year. It was done very quickly, he had left in a hurry." (p. 124)

Azad has a very lucid view of religion. For him, it is important to go to the mosque regularly, especially since his brother left: "I had been going to the mosque since my brother left. I found answers there. It was good for me" (p. 71). He does not see religion as an evil: everyone should be free to be interested in it or to turn away from it, without imposing their vision. This is what Azad reproaches his father for: "Basically, if the father had the job, maybe the brother wouldn't have left. The old man put religion aside, he never talked about it." (p. 71)

Nevertheless, even if religion is important to him, the young man is able to put things into perspective: "At the mosque, the preaching was a little bit out of place. Like on the news, the imam never told the world as it is. He wanted to be a poster star before he was a guide" (p. 72). He is well aware that in many ways the preaching of radicals reflects an exaggerated and harmful dogmatism.

The father has always been resistant to religion, probably because he lived in Syria during his childhood and adolescence. In his country, he witnessed a religious withdrawal that led to the worst conflicts. It is because of this trauma that he has always refused to inculcate religious practice in his children, and it is this aversion to religion that will indirectly give rise to the family drama: the death of his wife.

Through the characters of the father and the little brother, who are diametrically opposed, religious radicalisation is perfectly highlighted in this novel, as is the rise of indoctrination.

AVENUES FOR REFLECTION

A FEW QUESTIONS FOR FURTHER REFLECTION...

- What effect does the alternation of the two brothers' points of view have?

- In the novel, Big Brother says: "How can you find your way back when you don't know where you came from" (p. 72). Comment on this sentence in the context of the novel.

- Apart from being brothers, what kind of relationship do Big Brother and Little Brother have? Explain how they change in the course of the novel and why.

- What themes are dealt with in this novel? Explain how they make this novel very topical.

- Do you think the notion of religion is important in the novel?

- What are the views of the different characters on religion?

- Throughout the story, the author uses a mixture of slang and Arabic. Find some examples. Explain why this is significant in the context of the novel.

- How does this novel highlight the uberisation of society?

TO GO FURTHER

REFERENCE EDITION

GUVEN M., *Big Brother*, Paris, Éditions Philippe Rey, 2017.

BENCHMARK STUDIES

MARCU I. M., "The writing of 'outsider' authors. On the periphery of the norm", in *Carnets* (online), Second series – 7, 2016, https://journals.openedition.org/carnets/961.

DELAS D., « Les parlers jeunes dans deux romans littéraires » in *Cairn* (online), 2003, https://www.cairn.info/revue-le-francais-aujourd-hui-2003-4-page-89.htm.

Your opinion is important to us!
Leave a comment on the website of your online bookshop
and share your favourites on social networks!

www.brightsummaries.com

Ebook EAN: 9782808686709
Paperback EAN: 9782808698108
Legal Deposit: D/2023/12603/1090

Cover: © Primento
Digital conception by Primento, the digital partner of publishers.